DISNEY
PRINCESS
BEGINNINGS

MOANA'S Big Leap

BY SUZANNE FRANCIS

ILLUSTRATED BY THE
DISNEY STORYBOOK ART TEAM

Random House 🏠 New York

For the one and only Cath . . . Thanks, Mom.

—S. F.

rhcbooks.com

Library of Congress Cataloging-in-Publication Data
Names: Francis, Suzanne, author. | Disney Storybook Art Team,
    illustrator.
Title: Moana's big leap / by Suzanne Francis ; illustrated by the Disney
    Storybook Art Team.
Description: New York: Random House, [2019] | Series: Disney princess
    beginnings ; 7
Identifiers: LCCN 2019000946 | ISBN 978-0-7364-3794-3 (paperback) |
    ISBN 978-0-7364-8259-2 (lib. bdg.)
Subjects: BISAC: JUVENILE FICTION / Media Tie-In. | JUVENILE
    FICTION / Fairy Tales & Folklore / General. | JUVENILE FICTION /
    Social Issues / Friendship.
Classification: LCC PZ7.F8473 Mq 2019 | DDC [Fic]—dc23

Printed in the United States of America
10 9 8 7 6 5 4 3 2 1

Book design by Jenna Huerta & Betty Avila

This book has been officially leveled by using the F&P Text Level
Gradient™ Leveling System.

Random House Children's Books supports the First Amendment and
celebrates the right to read.

Chapter 1
A Future Chief

It was a cool morning on the island of Motunui, and Moana was busy. She worked to fasten two small bunches of bananas onto either end of a long pole. Her pet pig, Pua, napped by the trunk of a nearby tree.

"Almost ready," said Moana. Pua lazily opened his eyes, rolled onto his back, and stretched out. He smiled as he looked up at her.

Moana lifted the pole over her head and rested it across her shoulders. She knew her dad, Chief Tui, would be there soon, and she wanted to be ready. Pua hopped up and stood beside Moana, prepared to follow her anywhere.

As Tui crested a hill, he couldn't help but beam at the sight of his eight-year-old daughter carrying the bananas the way farmers did. "What do you have there?" he asked.

Moana grinned. "I thought I would bring them along as a treat for everyone," she explained.

"How thoughtful," said Tui. "Is it heavy?"

"Nope," Moana replied. "I've got it."

"Of course you do," her father said proudly.

As Tui led Moana through a grove of coconut trees, he told her about his plans for their rounds in the village. They would spend most of the day helping a family build a fale—a new home. Tui reminded Moana,

"It's a chief's duty to make sure the people of Motunui are happy. If there is a problem or if someone needs a hand, the chief is there to help."

Moana nodded in understanding. Her dad had been preparing her for her future role as chief since the day she was born. She loved Motunui and its people, and was proud to help them.

As they continued walking, it seemed as though every villager was talking about a big upcoming event: the Tiale celebration. It was held once every ten years in honor of their brave ancestor Tiale and the flower that was named for her. When Moana and her dad stopped to check in on an elder, Laumei, she gratefully accepted one of Moana's bananas and asked if Moana was excited about her first Tiale celebration.

"Yes!" answered Moana. "I'm *so* excited!"

"She has been counting the days," said Tui with a chuckle.

"I remember my first one," said Laumei, gazing off into the distance as if watching a memory play out before her. "Dancing, feasting, storytelling, the hunt for the Tiale flower, and then the competitions . . . You will love it!"

Soon Tui and Moana said goodbye to Laumei and continued on their rounds.

"When someone finds the flower, the competitions start the next day, right?" asked Moana.

Tui nodded. "That's right."

Earlier that morning, Tui had announced the events for the competitions: canoe racing, rock climbing, swimming, and cliff diving. Everyone interested in competing quickly made plans to train—including Moana.

"I can't wait to compete!" exclaimed Moana.

"I'm looking forward to cheering you on," said Tui.

"I can swim, paddle, and climb, but I don't know how to cliff dive," Moana said with a shrug. "The celebration starts tomorrow. Do you think I can learn in time?"

"If you work hard," said Tui. "*And* find a good teacher." Just then, they reached the family working on their new fale.

Tui greeted them, and Tautai, the father of the family, showed them around the site. "The holes are almost done, and we have the posts all ready," Tautai explained.

Tui was happy to hear it, and knew he and Moana would be able to help.

When Moana offered everyone a banana, they gratefully accepted. "Nice touch," said Toa, the family's grandmother.

Moana set down the bananas and joined

her dad. "You can hold the posts in place while we fill in the holes," he said.

Moana grabbed one of the posts and held it firmly as a villager from a nearby fale filled in the space around it with dirt, packing it down tightly. Pua planted himself beside her and munched on banana peels.

Moana and her dad worked for some time before continuing their walk through the village. Later that afternoon, while they helped a farmer secure one of his animal pens, Moana's friend Vailele approached. "Hi, Moana!" she said excitedly.

Moana waved energetically at Vailele, thrilled to see her. Pua rolled over at Vailele's

feet and stared up at her. She giggled and greeted him with a scratch.

"Want a banana?" Moana asked. "There are only a few left."

"Thanks," said Vailele, grabbing one. She peeled it and told Moana she was on her way to the shore. "Some of the villagers are making a big picture in the sand for the celebration." Vailele took a bite of banana. "Dee-licious!" she said with her mouth full.

"Oh yes!" said Moana. "Gramma Tala told me about that. I can't wait to see it."

"Once we finish here, you can go with Vailele to the shore and help," said Tui.

Grins spread across Moana's and Vailele's faces. "Thanks, Dad!" said Moana.

Moments later, the girls hurried off, with Pua trotting beside them.

"Can you believe the opening ceremony is *tomorrow*?" said Vailele, her eyes as big as coconuts.

"I know!" said Moana. "And then the search for the flower!"

"And once it's found . . ." Vailele looked at Moana with a sly smile.

"The competitions!" they cried in unison.

"I really want to try rock climbing," said Vailele. "But I have a tiny problem. Anything higher than . . . I don't know, my head? Well, it makes me feel like I have a rainstorm brewing inside my belly." She took a deep breath. "But in the spirit of Tiale, I will conquer my fear and find my bravery!" She raised her arms, as if showing off her muscles.

"You can do it," Moana said. Then she pointed to a nearby rock face. "That looks like a good place to practice."

Vailele nodded, ran toward it, and shouted at the rocks, "I'm going to climb you!" She placed one foot on a bulging rock, found a notch to grab, and lifted herself up.

Moana climbed alongside her while Pua stayed on the ground. The little pig stuck his snout into the dirt, looking for something interesting to eat or play with.

As they slowly made their way up, Moana explained that she was going to compete in at least three of the events. Then she added, "If I learn how to cliff dive in time, I'll do all four."

"If anyone can do it, it's you," said Vailele. "Okay. How high are we?" she asked, sounding a little exasperated.

"Let's see," said Moana, jumping down. She stood beside where Vailele was climbing. "Your foot is at my shoulder."

"That's it?" said Vailele, disappointed.

"Little by little," said Moana, "you'll get higher and higher." She picked up a small rock and gave it to Vailele. "Mark where your hand is and try to go above it next time."

"Good idea," said Vailele, scratching a line into the rock face.

Squeeee! Pua let out a loud squeal and shook his head.

"What's wrong?" Moana knelt down and giggled as she saw the source of his irritation. "Hold still," she cooed. All that digging in the dirt had left Pua with a beetle clinging to his snout. Moana picked up the bug, and it flew away.

"Is he okay?" asked Vailele, stepping back on the ground.

"It was a big scary beetle! Right, Pua?" Moana explained playfully. "But you were *very* brave." She comforted him with a pat. The little pig smiled proudly, then followed the girls toward the shore. When they reached the sand, Moana and Vailele both gasped. They couldn't believe their eyes.

Chapter 2
Surprises in the Sand

From the edge of the jungle, Moana and Vailele could see an incredible image on the shore. Thousands of little shells were carefully pressed into the sand, forming the outline of a giant flower.

Gramma Tala directed a bunch of villagers as they worked together to create the beautiful design. They were beginning to fill the outline, grouping the colors in patterns.

"You like it?" asked Gramma Tala.

"No," said Moana, "I love it!" She grinned at her grandmother and gave her a *hongi,* pressing their foreheads and noses together.

Moana spotted her mother sorting shells and sat down beside her. "Just wait until it's done," said Sina, smiling at Moana. "Your grandmother is doing a wonderful job."

Pua settled in the sand beside Moana and quickly fell asleep as Sina showed the girls what they could do to help. They gently pressed shells into the sand. "Not too deep," said Sina, demonstrating. "You want to press

them just right—so they're secure, but we can still see their beauty." Sina told the girls that each shell mattered. "Every one helps make the picture."

Moana and Vailele worked to press the shells into the sand just right and enjoyed watching the picture spring to life.

Moments later, Gramma Tala held up a small pink-and-white scallop shell and said, "We are going to need more of these." She asked Moana if she would like to join her in collecting them. "We can take the canoe." She picked up a large basket and pointed toward three jagged rocks rising out of the lagoon. "There should be more out there."

Moana never turned down the chance to go out on the water, and quickly agreed. She and Gramma Tala shared a deep love of the ocean and often spent time together dancing by its waves. Moana said goodbye to Vailele and ran over to a small canoe sitting in the sand.

Pua awoke and hopped into the boat as Moana dragged it into the lagoon. Gramma Tala waded beside Moana and soon climbed in. Moana gave the canoe a shove and joined her. Then she dipped her paddle into the water and headed toward the rocks.

"This is good practice for the race," Moana said.

Gramma Tala watched for a moment and said, "Remember to sit up straight. Shoulders back. Relaxed. And angle your paddle a bit more." Then she closed her eyes and enjoyed the quiet sound of the canoe moving swiftly across the water. "Good," she said, opening her eyes. She gently touched Moana's elbow, slightly lifting it. "There you go. Very good."

As Moana continued to paddle, she asked Gramma Tala to tell her about the Tiale celebrations she remembered.

"Let's see," said Gramma Tala, searching

her memory. "I remember colorful decorations, storytelling, and dancing, dancing, dancing."

"Did you ever compete?" asked Moana.

"I competed a little when I was much younger. But my favorite part of the celebration was always storytelling and dancing."

Moana nodded. "Of course," she said, not surprised. "I like those things, too."

"I know you do," said Gramma Tala. "You're my granddaughter. How could you not?"

Moana smiled.

"Your paddling? That's from your father," Gramma Tala said, watching Moana propel the canoe forward with her oar. "I think you're going to make us all very proud in the race."

"I hope so," said Moana. "I would love to try cliff diving, too. Do you know anyone who can teach me?"

"Hmm," said Gramma Tala, looking out at the water. "Maybe. Let's see you dive."

Gramma Tala and Pua watched as Moana carefully climbed up to the edge of the canoe and dove into the water. She swam to the surface and held on to the side of the boat, waiting for her review.

"Not bad," said Gramma Tala. "Bend your legs a bit more as you push off. That will help you dive farther. And relax your shoulders."

Moana pulled herself up and dove again. When she emerged, Gramma Tala said, "Very good. One more time." She grinned and added, "But this time, look for those little scallop shells while you're down there."

Moana climbed up and dove again, swimming to the seafloor. She spotted the shells, grabbed two handfuls, and swam to the surface. "Found them!" she said, raising her hands out of the water.

"Wonderful," said Gramma Tala.

Moana put the shells into the basket and held on to the side of the canoe, looking up at her grandmother thoughtfully. "Do *you* know how to cliff dive?"

Gramma Tala shook her head. "No. But I do know how to make a splash." Gramma Tala stood up and shouted, "Look out below!" She clutched her legs, hugging her knees, and jumped off the side of the canoe.

Moana giggled at the sight of her grandmother plunging into the water, sending up a big wave. When Gramma Tala surfaced, Moana cheered.

"Let's get some more shells," said Gramma Tala. She and Moana dove down and continued collecting, depositing the shells into the basket until it was full.

Soon they were back inside the canoe,

with Pua cheerfully sitting on the bow and Moana paddling toward shore. "So . . . did you think of anybody who can teach me to cliff dive?" Moana asked.

"Maybe," said Gramma Tala mysteriously. "Maybe."

Moana wondered why her grandmother wasn't giving her a straight answer. "Can you *maybe* tell me who?" she asked anxiously.

Gramma Tala's lips curled into a sly grin, and she said, "Let's bring the shells to the shore first."

Moana paddled even faster, picking up speed

as she tried to get back as quickly as possible. "Very good," said Gramma Tala.

When they arrived on the shore, Pua led the way as Moana and Gramma Tala brought the basket over to the group.

"Looks like you found plenty," said Sina, peering inside.

"Moana has a question for you," said Gramma Tala.

"I do?" asked Moana, looking confused.

"You should ask her what you asked me," said Gramma Tala. She turned her attention to the design and began telling everyone to make little adjustments here and there.

"What is it, Moana?" asked Sina.

"I want to find someone who can teach me to cliff dive," said Moana.

"Ask *her*," called Gramma Tala.

Moana was very confused but turned back to her mom and asked, "Will *you* teach me?"

Sina smiled. "Of course."

Moana had had no idea her mother knew how to cliff dive. "Did you compete?" she asked.

Fetuao, a village elder who was sifting shells nearby, chuckled and repeated, "Did she compete?" She looked at Moana and said, "Your mother was the greatest cliff diver I have ever seen. She was a champion!"

Sina laughed as she watched her daughter's chin nearly hit the sand. "Is it true?" Moana asked.

"Cliff diving was always my favorite activity," said Sina with a sneaky smile.

"She's modest," said Fetuao. "Ask anyone who is old enough to have seen her and they will tell you the same thing. She was the *best*."

Moana was speechless. She

looked at her mother and tried to imagine her high on a cliff, ready to dive off.

"The celebration starts tomorrow, so we better start your training soon," Sina said.

"Yes!" said Moana, jumping up and down with anticipation. "Thank you! Yes!" She gave her mother a big hug.

Sina laughed. "I'm excited, too," she said, hugging Moana back. "But for now, let's take care of these shells."

"Okay," said Moana, releasing her mother. She plopped down on the sand and tried to focus on helping.

Gramma Tala walked over to Moana

and knelt down beside her. "So you found yourself a teacher," she whispered. Moana nodded. Gramma Tala chuckled and patted her on the back. "Very good."

Chapter 3
The Celebration Begins

Later that night, when Moana and her dad were back home, she told him that she was going to learn to cliff dive. Tui raised his eyebrows. "Really?" he said. "So who is your teacher, then?"

Moana squinted as she stared at her father, trying to read his expression. "Do you have any guesses?" she asked.

Tui scratched his head. "Hmm. Who could it be?"

Moana gently poked his arm and asked, "Who do you think? Come on. One guess."

Sina appeared in the doorway as Tui shrugged his shoulders. "I give up. Who is this mysterious teacher?"

"Me," said Sina, grinning.

Tui looked at Sina with wide eyes, then back to Moana. "I didn't know your mother knew how to cliff dive!" he exclaimed.

"Neither did I!" said Moana. She paused and looked at her parents, who both held tight-lipped smiles for a moment before they burst out laughing. Moana narrowed her eyes at her father and said, "You did, Dad. You knew."

The three laughed together, and Tui nodded. "Yes, I did," he said, gazing lovingly at Sina. "How could I ever forget? Watching her was an *experience*." He turned to Moana. "I remember seeing your mother cliff dive for the first time when she was just about your age," he said, gently touching Moana's nose. "She was incredible. Standing up on Masina Cliff, perched like a magnificent bird."

Moana gasped and looked at her mother. "You dove off *Masina Cliff*?" she asked.

Sina chuckled and nodded. "That's where I used to practice."

Tui looked at Moana with his eyebrows raised. "Can you imagine?" His eyes sparkled as he continued to recall the fond memory. "She'd fearlessly leap off that sky-high cliff and soar toward the water like a giant bird, making barely a splash at the bottom. Amazing."

"Wow," whispered Moana, trying to picture it in her mind. She turned to her mother and asked, "Who taught you?"

"My mother," answered Sina. "She was a great cliff diver. I used to think she was fearless."

"Was she?"

Sina shook her head. "No," she replied. "But she practiced. A lot. And the more you practice, the more comfortable and confident you become. That's how she taught me. And that is how I will teach you." Sina gave Moana a *hongi*.

"After the opening ceremony tomorrow, everyone will start looking for the flower," said Moana. "Finding it usually takes a few days, right? Will I have enough time to learn how to cliff dive before the competition starts? What if—" Moana couldn't stop asking the questions that rapidly popped into her head.

"Slow down, slow down," said Sina. She explained that finding the flower was a challenge. "And yes—it usually takes at least a few days."

"No one has ever found it on the first night," Tui said. "The longest it ever took was eight days."

"But if we work hard, you'll learn in time," said Sina, putting a reassuring arm around Moana.

"Now we had all better get some sleep," said Tui. "We need to be rested for tomorrow."

Early the next morning, Moana awoke with the sunrise and bounced out of bed, ready for the day to begin. Everyone on the island got busy preparing for the celebration. Some put finishing touches on decorations, while dancers and musicians practiced. Colorful flowers were placed everywhere, and all the villagers wore garlands and crowns.

When it was finally time, drummers gathered on the shore and began banging out a bold rhythm. Dancers lined up along a path leading toward the shell design in the sand, and Chief Tui, Sina, and Moana, all wearing ceremonial dress, appeared at its start and began to slowly walk. Moana beamed as the music played and the dancers gestured toward her, swaying and smiling as she passed.

When the music stopped, Chief Tui addressed the crowd. "Today is a special day," he said. "It's the day we begin to celebrate our very brave ancestor Tiale." The villagers cheered, and Tui continued. "We always begin by listening to one of our elders share Tiale's story. To remind us why

we celebrate." Tui turned toward Gramma Tala with a big smile as he continued, "My favorite storyteller—my mother—will share it with us now." Gramma Tala stepped up beside Tui and gave him a *hongi.* Then he sat down with Moana and Sina, and everyone prepared to listen.

The drummers played a low, suspenseful rhythm as Gramma Tala scanned the crowd,

 capturing everyone's attention. "This legend begins in a place where none of us have ever been and likely will

never go: Lalotai!" Gramma Tala paused to let the spooky beat hang in the air before continuing. "The realm of monsters, as it is called, is far beyond the reef, beneath the ocean. Ferocious monsters of all shapes and sizes lurk, with their gnashing teeth and sharp claws. Millions of eyes seek out the weak and find those who try to hide!"

Some of the youngest children fearfully leapt into their parents' laps. One of them let out a tiny squeak, burying his face in his mother's arms. Moana held Pua close and leaned in, loving every second of Gramma Tala's dramatic presentation.

"Now, let us imagine going to this dark and terrible place," said Gramma Tala. "For that is where our story begins." The drummers banged a few final loud, enthusiastic beats, and she began to tell Tiale's story.

Chapter 4
The Legend of Tiale

Many, many years ago, in Lalotai, a monster heard the cries of a baby and rose to the surface to investigate. When the monster emerged, she discovered an abandoned human baby girl. A mortal. It came as a complete surprise, but the monster somehow felt that she should protect the baby. Knowing the other monsters would not feel the same — they would most certainly destroy any human of any age—the monster adopted the baby girl as her own and kept her hidden inside a large seashell down in Lalotai.

The monster couldn't always calm the baby's cries, so it wasn't long before the others found out about her secret. They were angry and quickly set out to find the baby. Aware that she could not fight all the monsters on her own, the "mother" monster clutched the baby and her shell and blasted out of Lalotai. She looked up to see a bright full moon hanging in the sky. Although she didn't want to let the baby go, she begged the guardian of the moon to take her to safety and raise her as her own.

The moon guardian had never seen a monster beg, and she had certainly never seen one try to help a mortal. She watched in amazement as the monster desperately pushed a wall of dried coral in front of the seashell, trying her best to disguise it. Then the monster jumped high into the air and splashed back down into the sea, leading the other monsters away from the baby.

Impressed by the strength of this strange mother's love, the moon guardian agreed to grant her wish and care for the child.

The monsters quickly destroyed the mother monster, leaving behind nothing but a single eye. This was to ensure that she would witness the end of the baby girl once the monsters tracked her down.

Keeping the girl inside the seashell, the moon guardian whisked her away to a beautiful island called Motunui. She named the girl Tiale.

Tiale grew up to be brave, strong, and clever. She worked hard to support and help the village. She loved Motunui and its people with all her heart. And they loved her for it.

The moon guardian had taught Tiale to stay away from the water. She had told her about the monsters and Lalotai, so she understood the risk of going near the sea, where monsters might find her.

One day, Tiale broke the rule. A terrible storm hit, and Tiale heard the cries of fishers out at sea. Without a second thought, she bravely got into a canoe and paddled out, abandoning the moon guardian's warning and risking her life in an attempt to save the fishers.

But it was a terrible trap. The monsters had discovered where Tiale had been living and tricked her into the sea. Inside the boat were not fishers—but monsters in disguise. When she reached them, the monsters pulled Tiale down to Lalotai.

That night, when the moon guardian discovered Tiale was missing, she was furious. She cast a moonbeam into the sea. When its glow hit the seafloor, it formed a magical shark that went in search of Tiale. The shark swam for many days. When it finally found Tiale in Lalotai, she was weak from fighting. The shark carried her out of the realm of monsters and brought her to the moon guardian. To preserve the courageous girl and her beautiful spirit, the moon guardian turned her into a rare and lovely white flower.

The mysterious Tiale flower blossoms every ten years. It can only be found high on the tallest mountains of Motunui, far from monsters. The flower stays closed during the day, remaining hidden, and blooms at night so the moon guardian can gaze upon her.

Chapter 5
The Big Bright Moon

As she finished the tale, Gramma Tala paused, letting it wash over the crowd. Then she said, "That is why we celebrate Tiale. For her bravery and dedication to our island. Tiale reminds us that everyone who lives on Motunui is family."

Then Gramma Tala announced that she had prepared a simple, fun dance and invited everyone to join in. "Every dance tells a story, and in this one, we will scare the monsters away from Tiale and order them to stay in Lalotai," she said with a playful grin.

Moana and Vailele looked at each other excitedly as they rose and joined the group following Gramma Tala to the shallow water.

Drummers began to play as Gramma Tala demonstrated the steps. The dance was energetic, with villagers splashing around in the water, stomping their feet, and slapping the surface of the sea. Moana loved every second, and the ocean waves seemed to play along with her, rushing the shore and retreating to the beat of the music.

One final splash and everyone cheered.

"Let's do it again!" exclaimed Moana, beaming.

"One more time!" Gramma Tala shouted. "But faster!"

The dancers chuckled as the drummers banged out a speedier rhythm, and they attempted to do the steps even faster, splashing and stomping and laughing the whole time. When the drummers hit their final beat, everyone cheered and hugged each other, exhilarated by the performance.

Soon it was time for the feast. The men had already built and heated the underground oven. They were roasting fish, bananas, taro, and coconut.

Bagock! Heihei, the silly village chicken, squawked as he walked toward the hot coals for what seemed like the fifteenth time that day. One of the villagers scooted him back and said, "Should we just cook him? Maybe he *wants* to be food."

"Aw. Maybe he's hungry," said Moana. She led him away from the oven and put a piece of papaya in front of him. Heihei pecked at the ground, missing the sweet fruit every time.

Soon after the meal, torches lit up the night and a big round moon hung in the sky. Tui announced that it was time to search for the flower. "This is a challenge," he said. "Whoever finds the Tiale flower is said to be brave. It is tradition for the last person who found the flower to share their tale." Then he introduced Pilifeai.

"I searched every night," Pilifeai said, facing the crowd. "Nobody could find the flower. But on the fourth night of the celebration . . . I found it!" He pointed toward

a mountain in the distance. "Over there. A fat lizard was scurrying in the brush." He mimicked the sound of rustling leaves and twigs as he raised his eyebrows and flashed his tongue, pretending to be a lizard. "I followed him . . . and then I saw it." His eyes popped wide as he continued to describe the flower. "Its big white petals peeked out over the rocks—the blooms kind of glowed with a tint of blue at their edges and each one was about the size of my palm." He held up his hand, showing off its size. "The flowers were on leafy green stems." His face broke into a jolly smile and he added, "I felt so happy to have found it and was so proud when I carefully picked one and brought it back to the village."

Tui asked if he had any advice for those joining in the search. Pilifeai thought for a moment and said, "Be patient, have fun, and . . . listen for lizards!"

Tui thanked him for sharing his memory

and gestured to Tautai, who was holding a large conch shell. "This will signal the end of the search each night." Tautai demonstrated, blowing a three-note pattern. Tui went on to explain that a different pattern would let everyone know when the flower had been found. Tautai demonstrated again, this time blowing five notes.

Tui's eyes sparkled as he looked up at the night sky. "The moon is big and bright," he said. "So the search for the Tiale flower begins!"

Chapter 6
The Search Begins

While the moon cast its silver glow, dozens of villagers set off in search of the precious flower.

Moana ran up to her mother. "Will you come with me?" she asked.

"Yes, I would love to," said Sina. The two walked toward the jungle together. "You lead the way, my brave warrior. I will follow you."

Moana looked around before saying, "This way." With Pua at her side, she confidently headed toward the foot of one of the island's many mountains. "Did you ever find the flower?" she asked her mother.

Sina shook her head. "No, but I looked every night. Sometimes with my family, some nights with my friends. I had so much fun searching," she said. "It was an adventure." Sina explained how she enjoyed finding other things—beautiful rocks and branches or twigs twisted in interesting shapes. "Walking around the island at night and searching . . . it made everything look different."

As they continued, Sina described hearing a loud thump while searching with a friend. "It made us both jump," she said. "Then we saw what made the noise. It was the largest bat I have ever seen—to this day. It was huge!" Sina widened her arms to an impossibly large size, and she and Moana laughed.

Moana had never been in the mountains so late—she was usually at home or even fast asleep by this time. She quickly understood what her mother meant about the search at night making things look different. At first, everything was colorless, quiet, and still. But the farther they walked, the more Moana noticed. They passed big misshapen boulders

and massive trees that looked like monsters. When she listened carefully, she heard a night chorus of birds and bugs echoing through the jungle. And when the wind made the trees sway, their shadows seemed to dance to the tune of rustling leaves. Pua, who had also never been out so late, stayed close to Moana, no longer feeling the urge to stray and explore.

Moana gazed at the glistening stars covering the sky and marveled at how they seemed to stretch all the way down to the dark, distant mountains. Suddenly, something on a nearby peak caught her eye.

"Look!" she said, pointing toward the white object. "It could be the flower! Come on!" Moana darted up toward it as fast as she could, Pua pouncing after her.

Sina chuckled and ran after her, calling, "I'm coming!" Moana was far ahead before Sina finally crested the peak.

"Not the Tiale flower," said Moana with a

sigh. "Not even a flower! It's a white feather."

Sina laughed. "It's a pretty one," she said. "Still a good find."

"It is," agreed Moana. "Let's go this way." She used the feather to point toward a slender path that wove through some towering banyan trees. Their gnarled roots stretched out like snakes in the darkness. Moana and her mother walked carefully to avoid tripping.

Soon the conch horn's bellowing tune rang out, and they stopped to listen. "Three notes," said Moana. "That means everyone will search again tomorrow night, right?"

Sina nodded. "Correct. But before that,

in the morning, *you* are learning how to cliff dive."

"Yes!" cheered Moana. "I can't wait." She and Sina turned around and headed back toward the village.

Chapter 7
The Big Leap

Moana was ready bright and early the next morning. She followed her mother out of the village and up to Masina Cliff. When they reached the pool of water at its foot, Sina said, "Stay down here so you can watch me." Then she climbed up, up, up to the very top.

Moana didn't blink as Sina gracefully walked to the edge of the cliff. She remembered her father saying how her mother looked like a magnificent bird perched and waiting.

Sina raised her arms as she prepared for the dive. Bending her knees, she sprang off the cliff and sailed through the air, just like a graceful bird. She broke the surface of the water with hardly a splash.

When Sina emerged, Moana hopped as she clapped and cheered wildly. "Amazing! Just like Dad said!" she exclaimed. "I want to do that!"

Sina smiled as she swam toward Moana. "That was fun," she said. "Could you tell how far away from the cliff I jumped?"

"Yes," said Moana, her head still spinning from the spectacle.

"That's important," said Sina. "I'm going to do it again. Watch the line my body makes as it goes toward the water. I stay firm and strong, but relaxed."

Moana took note as Sina dove off the cliff again, paying special attention to her body. Then she asked if she could try.

"Yes," said Sina. "But first we'll start a little lower." She pointed to a boulder that jutted out, just above the lagoon.

Moana wrinkled her nose. "The boulder?" she

asked, sounding a little disappointed.

"We start out slow and work up to Masina Cliff," Sina explained as she led the way.

Moana understood. "That's just what I told Vailele to do with her climbing." She wondered how her friend was doing and if she had been practicing.

Moana scaled the boulder, raised her arms, and dove into the lagoon. When she surfaced, Sina said, "Try it again. This time I want you to make sure your arms are straight and near your ears when you hit the water."

Moana nodded and tried again.

"Better," Sina said. "Try to relax your shoulders. Make sure they don't creep up toward your ears."

Moana dove several more times, adjusting her body to her mother's suggestions until Sina clapped her hands and shouted, "Perfect! Now let's walk."

Moana followed Sina up to a cliff, slightly higher than the boulder. She stood at its edge, looked down at the water, and smiled. Her smile widened as she sprang off and dove into the water, making a big *SPLASH!*

"Make sure you spring *out* and *away* from

the cliff," said Sina as Moana emerged. "And take note of the space between the cliff and the water."

Moana nodded. "Okay. I'll try again," she said, rushing back up.

Sina watched as Moana dove again. "Good," she said.

Over the next few days, Sina and Moana went to Masina Cliff together as Sina continued to teach her how to cliff dive. Moana loved climbing higher and higher as she got better and better. She worked hard to remember everything Sina taught her and practiced

every chance she got. It felt great knowing that with each dive, she was getting closer to the top of the mountain.

Moana spent her days focused on cliff diving, and every night, she searched for the flower, going with Vailele and a few other friends one night and with Gramma Tala another. Still, the nights passed and nobody had found it.

On the morning of the fifth day, Moana dove into the water from a fairly high cliff and emerged. "How was that? How were my legs? Were they straight? My arms? Shoulders?" Moana asked, eagerly awaiting her mother's critique.

Sina looked deep into Moana's eyes and said, "You're ready."

Moana squealed and wrapped her wet arms around her mom, bouncing with excitement. She couldn't believe it: she was finally going to dive off Masina Cliff!

When the two climbed up to the top, Sina said, "Remember everything you have learned."

Moana nodded and stepped toward the cliff's edge. She looked down at the sparkling blue water rippling in the pool far below.

Suddenly, a strange tingling feeling pulsed through her body. She couldn't believe it—she was nervous.

"It's completely normal to be a little anxious," said Sina, as if reading Moana's mind. "You just have to breathe and center yourself."

"Breathe and center myself," Moana repeated, inhaling deeply.

"Your bravery and skill will shine through," added Sina.

Moana waited a few more moments, searching for her courage. She bent her knees and raised her arms, but when she went to dive, she couldn't. She was afraid.

"I will teach you another trick," Sina said. "Yell."

"Huh?"

"You take a deep breath, collect all those nerves and fear, ball it up, and shout it out! I used to shout, 'GO!' And then I would . . . go." Sina reached for Moana's hand. "You can do it," she said. "It's in your blood."

Moana nodded, ready to try again. She closed her eyes as she inhaled and exhaled calmly. Looking out, she raised her arms, bent her knees . . . and shouted at the top of her lungs, "GO!" Then she sprang off the cliff!

Time seemed to slow as she soared like a giant bird. The air was cool against her skin, and she felt like she was flying. When her fingertips touched the surface of the pool, she plunged in and swam to the bottom. She pushed off the rocky floor with her feet and rose back to the surface, wearing a smile so big her cheeks ached.

Sina clapped and yelled, "That was beautiful!"

Moana hooted and hollered, splashing her arms against the water as she screamed, "That. Was. Amazing!"

Sina laughed as she watched Moana swim to the shore and scramble back up to the top of the cliff, ready to dive again.

Chapter 8
Plans and Adventures

Later that day, Moana found Vailele and asked how she was doing with her climbing. Vailele grinned and led Moana to the rock face where she had marked how high she'd climbed each day. Now it had many scratch marks on it, reaching nearly to the top!

"Wow," said Moana. "That's great!"

Vailele started climbing up the rock. "Just like you said, I kept going higher and higher," she explained, slowly pulling herself up. "If I could just go a little farther . . ." She stretched and stepped even higher.

"One more step and you're past your last mark," said Moana. "You're *soooo* close. Try taking deep breaths. . . . And yelling helps," she offered, repeating her mother's advice.

"Yelling . . . ," said Vailele, thinking it over. Suddenly, she let out a loud *"Ahhhhh!"* and managed another step. "It worked!" she exclaimed. "But I'm getting a little nervous." She looked down. Then she slowly lowered herself and asked, "How's cliff diving going?"

"Do you want to see?" Moana asked eagerly.

Vailele nodded and the two friends set off together. They neared the base of Masina Cliff, and Vailele looked up in awe. The towering cliff seemed to touch the clouds. "You dove off *that*?"

Moana giggled. "Uh-huh," she said. "I was really nervous at first, but each time I did it, it got easier. Wanna see the view from the top?"

Vailele nodded and followed Moana up the winding path.

"Whoa," Vailele said, taking in the view. Then she watched as Moana walked to the cliff's edge, centered herself, shouted, and dove. When Moana emerged, Vailele clapped her hands and shouted, "I can't believe you just did that!"

As Moana swam to the shore, Vailele peered over the opposite edge of the cliff and saw a rock face stretching all the way to the ground. It was quite a drop but full of ledges and perfect for climbing. Vailele thought if she climbed *down* the rock face, maybe it would make her fear of climbing *up* disappear. She held on to some ledges and slowly lowered herself.

Moana hiked back up to the top of the cliff and was surprised to find that her friend had disappeared. "Vailele?" she said.

"Down here," called Vailele.

Moana followed Vailele's voice and looked down to see her clinging to the rock face below. Vailele shared her plan, suggesting Moana meet her at the bottom. "Maybe this will make me brave," she added.

The sky was darkening, and Moana shivered as a chill in the air snapped against her skin. "It's getting late," she said. "I think we should stick together." She didn't want to make Vailele nervous, but it felt like a storm was coming. If the rock face got wet, it would be very slippery.

Vailele lowered herself to a small landing that was big enough to stand on, the perfect place for a little break. She shook out her arms and looked down, realizing how much farther she had to go. Rain began falling from the sky, and a tingling fear shot through her body. "Oh no!" she said. "Why did I do this?"

Thinking fast, Moana grabbed a long vine from a nearby tree. She secured it and

gave it a tug, testing its weight. Holding on
to the vine, she rappelled toward Vailele.
"I'm coming down!" she shouted.

Vailele screeched as the rain poured

down and the wind picked up. Terrified, she clung to the rock face.

When Moana reached her, the friends huddled together, shielding each other from the wind and rain as it whipped and swirled around them. "It's too slippery," Moana shouted. She looked around, searching for a way to get down safely.

A big old moss-covered tree growing out of the base of a nearby mountain gave her an idea. One of its thick mossy branches arched over a small ravine, stretching up toward the rock face like a finger. The end of the branch nearly touched a landing below. If they could get down to the next level, they could get to the branch.

Moana pointed to the landing. "If we can get down there, then we can slide along the branch to the other mountain," she explained.

"What?" cried Vailele, not liking the sound of Moana's plan.

But Moana had already figured out how they could do it. "The vine is long enough to get us down. I'll go first," she said.

"But—" Vailele started.

"We can do this. It'll be okay," Moana assured her. "We'll do it together."

Vailele nodded, and Moana lowered

herself. "See. Not so bad," she said. "Your turn."

Vailele gripped the vine. She screamed as the wind wobbled it this way and that.

"Hold on tight!" Moana shouted. She held the bottom of the vine as Vailele inched her way down it. "Almost there," she said, reaching up and gently touching Vailele's foot. "See?"

Finally, Vailele made it to the landing beside Moana. As the rain continued to pour, Moana took the vine and rubbed it against a jagged rock, sawing off a lengthy piece. "Ready to go for a little ride?" she shouted, grinning.

Vailele winced. She watched Moana reach up and throw the wet vine over the mossy tree branch. Moana told Vailele that they were both going to hold on tightly to the vine. "Our weight will make it slide down the branch," she explained. "Ready?"

"I don't know—" started Vailele.

Moana held the piece of vine with both hands and shouted, "Hold on tight and don't look down!" Vailele grabbed the vine, putting her hands next to Moana's. "Let's yell first," said Moana, noticing the fear on her friend's face.

"Ahhhh!" they shouted.

"Now we're going to jump. One . . . two . . . three . . . GO!"

Gripping the vine and yelling the whole way, they leapt off the ledge. The vine slipped down the wet tree branch, carrying them toward the base of the mountain. Moana stretched her legs out and hit the trunk of the tree with her feet, slowing them to a stop. As their yelling turned to laughter, the two climbed down. "Ground!" Vailele cheered, gratefully looking at the jungle floor and holding her arms out as if giving it a hug.

Moana spotted a little cave under an overhang. "Come on," she said, grabbing Vailele's hand and leading her to it.

"I don't think I've ever been so scared in my whole life," whispered Vailele, trying to catch her breath.

"You were brave to try to climb down the rock face," said Moana.

"Maybe my plan did work. Maybe I'll climb higher than anyone," she said with a grin. "Or . . . maybe I'll never climb again."

The rain continued to slap against the mountainside, and the friends sat huddled together, watching it stream down in front of them like a little waterfall.

Once the wind quieted, the sound of the rain began to slow, and soon it was nothing but a mist. Moana and Vailele stepped out of the cave and looked around. The moon was shining, and everything looked silver and magical. Without the noise of the raindrops, the jungle was especially calm and quiet.

Moana noticed something glowing through the mist in the near distance. "Look over there," she said, pointing.

As the mist cleared, Vailele saw it and nearly fell over. Without a word, the girls hurried toward the white glow, both wondering if it could be the Tiale flower.

Chapter 9
Beautiful Flowers

Moana and Vailele made their way across the wet, slippery terrain until they finally saw several leafy green stems springing out of the rocks . . . each one supporting a large white flower!

The girls sat beside the mysterious plant, inspecting it. The moonlight touched the white blossoms, tinting their curved edges with a hint of blue. Raindrops had collected on the large petals and sparkled like crystals.

"I don't believe it," whispered Vailele.

"The Tiale flower," Moana said. She leaned toward one of them and breathed in its light, sweet scent.

They sat in silence for a moment, admiring the lovely sight. Moana thought about the story of Tiale and imagined the moon guardian happily watching from

above. She looked up, briefly searching the sky for the guardian's smiling face, before gazing back down at the flower, taken with its unique beauty.

They each plucked a flower and headed home to share the news. Soon the conch shell's five notes rang out, letting everyone know the Tiale flower had been found!

The girls told Moana's parents about what had happened. "I'm so glad you are safe," Tui said. "You are both very brave."

Hearing those words from the chief put a shy smile on Vailele's face.

"You get to wear your Tiale flower," explained Sina. "It's a symbol of your bravery.

I'm proud of you girls." She helped them put the flowers in their hair.

Once everyone had gathered, Moana and Vailele stood by Tui and Sina as Tui announced, "Moana and Vailele have had a very interesting night out in the storm, and they have found the Tiale flower!" Everyone cheered. "So the competitions start tomorrow!" Tui shouted.

Moana and Vailele's friends rushed over, congratulating them, admiring the flowers, and asking questions. Gramma Tala stepped forward and said, "You can hear all about it in the morning, but for now, everyone should get their rest for the competitions."

Vailele spotted her parents and gave Moana a giant hug before running over to them.

"What a night," whispered Gramma Tala, putting her arms around Moana. "You found the Tiale flower!"

Moana sleepily smiled up at her grandmother, feeling proud and completely exhausted. The two walked with Sina and Tui beside them. Once they got home, Moana fell fast asleep.

The next day, musicians played while the villagers gathered, ready for the competitions to start. Vailele and Moana, both wearing their flowers, led everyone to the shore for the first event: canoe racing.

Participants pulled their canoes across the sand to the starting line as the rest of the villagers prepared to cheer them on.

Pua hopped into Moana's canoe as she pulled it into the water. "We've got this, Pua," she said, smiling at the happy pig.

Once everyone was lined up and ready, Tui announced, "The canoe race goes over to the east end of the island." He pointed into the distance and continued, "Racers will go around the boulder where Tautai is." Tui waved at Tautai, and he waved back. Everyone cheered as the race began.

Moana dipped her paddle into the water and took off toward the boulder. Pua sat in the back of the canoe with his head up, enjoying the feeling of the ocean breeze flapping his ears.

Bagock! Moana frowned as she slowed and looked around, searching for the source of the sound. *Bagock!* Heihei, that silly chicken, bobbed up and down, flailing around in the sea!

"Heihei!" Moana cried, scooping him

up with her paddle. "How did you—? *Why* did you—?" But she just shook her head, knowing she wasn't going to get an answer. She dumped the chicken into the canoe. Pua squealed and dove into her lap. "Okay," she said. "This is not going to work." She nudged Pua off her lap and told them both to stay still and calm. "Just until we get to the shore," she added, wondering why she was trying to reason with a pig and a chicken.

Moana looked out at all the racers ahead of her and paddled as hard as she could.

Tui, Sina, and Gramma Tala watched as Moana's canoe glided across the water and rounded the boulder in the distance. When Gramma Tala squinted, she noticed some colorful feathers in the boat. "Is that . . . Heihei?" she asked.

Sina and Tui stared, straining to see. Then they saw Heihei hop up on top of Pua's head! "That would be a yes," said Sina. "Heihei is riding inside Moana's canoe. On top of Pua's head."

"And yet . . . look how focused she is," Tui said proudly.

Soon Moana and several others were heading toward the finish line. Pua's ears hung low as he sat as still as a statue, staring up at the wet chicken perched on his head.

"We're almost there, Pua," Moana said. She knew the little pig was trying his best to help.

Moana saw some other racers cross the finish line before her as she paddled with all her might, getting closer and closer.

"Yes!" she shouted as she made it across. She pulled her canoe to shore, and Pua leapt straight into her arms, causing Heihei to flap his wings and flop onto the sand. Moana cradled Pua and patted him lovingly while Heihei clucked and pecked at the side of the canoe. Moana's family rushed up to congratulate her.

"Very good," said Gramma Tala. "Even with that distracting chicken in your boat!"

Tui and Sina hugged their daughter. "You make us all so very proud," Tui said, giving her a *hongi*.

Later that afternoon, everyone gathered around a wide rock face at the edge of the jungle for the next event: rock climbing. Tui handed each participant a small rock and explained, "Climb your highest, and scratch your name into the rock face to mark it."

Vailele and Moana took starting places beside each other. They tucked their rocks into their pockets and prepared to begin.

Moana faced the wall and shouted, "We're going to climb you!" Then she turned to her friend, grinning. "Right, Vailele?"

"Yes. We. Are," Vailele said, tapping her finger against the rock. She turned to Moana and added, "No rain and wind . . . where's the challenge?"

Moana chuckled and said, "I know, right? Too easy."

The competition began, and the participants made their way up the rock face. Vailele kept pace with Moana, and they continued to look over at each other, smiling along the way, having a blast. They

managed to get very high and scratched their names into the rock before heading back down.

Everyone cheered as the climbers landed on the ground.

"That's the highest I've ever climbed!" said Vailele, looking up at her mark.

"I guess your plan on the mountain *did* work," said Moana with a smile.

During the feast that night, everyone talked about the competitions. They were all looking forward to tomorrow's events: swimming and cliff diving.

Chapter 10
A Mother's Daughter

The next day, Moana readied to compete in the swimming event. The swimmers lined up in the lagoon as Tui explained they would race to Tautai, who stood on top of a sandbar in the distance. "You'll swim out to Tautai's little island, and the finish line will be back here," said Tui.

The race began, and Moana took off, swimming toward the sandbar. She focused on her strokes and was moving fast. It almost felt as if the ocean was pushing her along. Before she knew it, she had reached the sandbar and was turning around, swimming back toward the shore. She was in the lead!

Tui and Sina clapped, watching Moana swim toward the finish line.

Gramma Tala hooted and hollered, "Moana!"

"Go, Moana! Go!" shouted Vailele, jumping and splashing in the shallow water.

Her family erupted in applause as Moana crossed the finish line. She swam to shore and ran onto the sand, hugging her family and friends. Pua ran circles around her heels, until she picked him up for a cuddle.

Later that afternoon was the final event: cliff diving. The chosen cliff was almost as high as Masina Cliff and stood way above the lagoon by the beach. Tui encouraged the spectators to watch from the shore while the divers climbed to the top.

Sina gave her daughter a few encouraging words before Moana headed up. "Remember what you have learned. And don't forget to have fun, my little minnow," she said with a smile.

The divers lined up, ready to go one at

a time. Moana waited, watching the others dive off with confidence. She wondered if they felt any fear.

When it was her turn, she stepped up to the edge of the cliff and felt her heart beating fast. Taking a deep breath, she calmly centered herself and slowly raised her arms over her head. She shouted, "GO!" and dove off the cliff toward the sparkling ocean below.

Sina watched with pride as Moana gracefully soared into the water, leaving barely a splash. Fetuao, who was sitting nearby, said, "Oh, she looks just like you!"

Tui put his arm around Sina. "Her mother's daughter," he said proudly.

Gramma Tala leaned over and said, "Just like her mother!"

The family watched Moana swim toward the shore. She ran up onto the sand, grinning from ear to ear, and they wrapped her in a giant hug.

"Wonderful!" said Tui. "I can hardly believe my eyes."

"That was beautiful," said Sina.

Fetuao craned her neck and shouted, "You look just like your mother did!"

"Thank you," said Moana. It filled her with pride to hear those words. "I had the best teacher." She gave her mother another big hug and whispered in her ear, "Thank you, Mom."

That night, the villagers enjoyed the biggest feast yet. With plenty of food, music, and dancing, everyone had a wonderful time. After the feast, Chief Tui led the villagers to the location of the closing ceremony—where the Tiale flower had been discovered.

Moana and Vailele were thrilled to lead the way into the jungle and up the mountain. When they arrived at the place where they had found the flower, everyone quietly admired the sight. With even more Tiale blooms open, it was stunning. Big beautiful moths hovered around the many flowers, landing on their petals and sipping from their centers. Pua watched nervously as one of the moths landed on his snout before fluttering off and finding a flower.

Gramma Tala announced that there was one final part of Tiale's story to tell. She

waited for everyone to quiet down before beginning.

"As the moon guardian saw the Tiale flower bloom, it filled her with joy and pride. She truly loved Tiale and was happy to gaze upon her spirit once again. But then she thought of the monster from Lalotai who had brought her Tiale all those years ago. And sadness filled her heart. She marveled as she recalled how the monster had given up her life for the mortal baby. The moon guardian admired this selfless act and wanted to honor it. As a gift of thanks, respect, and appreciation, she gave the monster's remaining eye wings and turned it into the night moth. Now the monster, too, could continue to see Tiale and visit her in the moonlight."

The villagers stood around the flowers for another few moments, watching the moths fluttering and flickering in the pale light of the moon.

Soon everyone walked back down the mountain, heading home.

"I have something for you," said Sina, pulling Moana aside. "It is something to help you remember your first Tiale celebration and all the wonderful moments you have had."

"I don't think I could ever forget it," said Moana.

Sina smiled and told her daughter to hold out her wrist. "I am so impressed with all the wondrous things you do. You continue to bring your family honor and make us proud," she said.

Then she fastened a bracelet around Moana's wrist. Several objects were woven into it, and Sina pointed out each one, explaining its significance. There were shells from the design they had made in the sand, the white feather Moana had found the first night of the search, a pebble from the pool

of water below Masina Cliff, and petals from
the Tiale flower.

"I love it," said Moana. "And I love you."
She gave her mother a *hongi*. "Thank you for
teaching me how to cliff dive."

"It is my joy to be your teacher," said Sina, giving her daughter a big hug.

Pua leaned against Moana's leg, begging her to pick him up. "You need me to carry you home, you sleepy little pig?" said Moana, chuckling and scooping him up.

Tui and Gramma Tala joined them, and the family walked down the mountain together, sharing memories from the celebration they knew they would keep in their hearts forever.

EVERY PRINCESS HAS A STORY.
EVERY STORY HAS A BEGINNING.

Disney
PRINCESS
BEGINNINGS

Embark on new adventures with the girls
who will one day become princesses!